This Book Belongs To:

Sarah Seifert

FAVORITE PLAYTIME TALES

CHECKERBOARD PRESS

NEW YORK

CONTENTS

Copy-Kitten

No one knew
what the Copy-Kitten
really looked like—
Because he always
tried to look like
some other animal.

Sometimes he copied the pigs—

Sometimes he copied
the chickens—

But he never copied his mother—
As the other kittens did—

And his mother was worried
about him.

One day—

The circus came to town.

The kitten stole away to watch.

He crawled under the big tent.

First he looked at
the elephant—
The elephant was easy to copy.

Copying the lion was easy,
because the kitten looked
a little like a lion anyway.

But when Copy-Kitten
came to the giraffe—
And tried to stretch his neck
to look like HIM—
He couldn't do it, although he
tried and tried.

He stretched his neck,
he twisted his head—

He pushed his head
with his paws—
But he just couldn't look a bit
like the giraffe.
The poor kitten stopped trying—
He had never felt so sad
in his life.
He was so sad
and disappointed
that he made up his mind
never to copy anyone again.

When he was home again
everyone was very glad
to see him—

And everyone
was even more glad,
because the Copy-Kitten
wasn't copying anyone.

But his mother was still
worried about him—

Because he wouldn't copy her,
as the other kittens did.

All the other young animals copied their mothers—

But the Copy-Kitten
was too happy,
just being himself at last,
to copy anyone at all!

Teddy Bear
of
Bumpkin Hollow

TEDDY was a little brown bear. He was just about the cutest little brown bear that ever lived in Bumpkin Hollow. But he had one very bad habit. No matter what his mama told him to do—he wanted to do just the opposite.

If Mama Bear said, "Teddy, it's time to come in and eat lunch now," Teddy would stay right where he was and play and play.

If Mama Bear said, "Teddy, it's time to go to sleep now," he would just open his eyes as wide as wide and say, "But, Mama, I'm not sleepy."

No matter what Mama wanted him to do, he didn't want to do it. Why, if Mama told him to be a good boy and smile, he would make the most awful face. It was enough to scare Sammy Squirrel right out of his skin. Even Willie Woodpecker stopped pecking

holes in the White Pine tree and hid his head under his left wing when Teddy made a face like that.

Mama and Papa Bear talked about Teddy's strange behavior one evening after Teddy was asleep.

"What will we do!" Papa Bear said.

Mama Bear thought a long time. Finally she said, "I know *exactly* what to do. Teddy loves to visit Grandma and Grandpa Bear. We shall go there tomorrow morning.

But we shall wait and see if Teddy goes
or if Teddy stays at home."

"But he can't stay alone," said Papa.

"No, but Cousin Amanda will be glad to
stay with him, I know," said Mama.

Early the next morning Mama called to Teddy, "Hurry, Teddy, the sun is up and it is time for little bears to be up, too."

Teddy didn't even grunt.

Mama called him again, but still he didn't wake up.

Mama had to call him six times because, of course, he didn't want to do anything he was told to do.

After breakfast Mama gave him a shiny red bucket. "Go over to Honey Bee Hive," she said, "and get this bucket full of the very best Mountain Flower Honey.

"Take the short path and not the long one through the Green Woods," she warned. "Now hurry, Teddy. If you are back by ten o'clock, you will have a very pleasant surprise. If you are not back by then, you will be very sorry."

"What is the surprise?" asked Teddy. Teddy just loved surprises.

"I can't tell you now," said Mama, "or it wouldn't be a surprise any longer. Now run along, and remember, *don't go through the woods.*"

Teddy ran down the path swinging the shiny red bucket. Soon he came to the little twisted path that went into the woods.

Teddy stopped. How he did love to go through the Green Woods and wade in the icy mountain stream!

"Oh, dear," said Teddy. "What shall I do? I wonder what the old surprise is anyway. I'll run as fast as I can. Then it won't take me any longer to go through the woods than to go by the short path."

And Teddy scampered down the little twisted path into the Green Woods. Soon he came to the icy mountain stream.

"I'll just take a minute to splash in it," he said to himself. Then he saw Mr. Bull Frog on a rock.

"Good morning," croaked Mr. Frog. "I'm so glad to see you, Teddy Bear. I have been

learning a new song. Do sit down and listen
and tell me what you think of it."

Teddy sat down on the cool green bank
and wiggled his toes in the icy water.

Mr. Frog croaked his very loudest.
"That is a very fine song," said Teddy.
"Let me sing you another," said Mr. Frog.
"No," said Teddy, suddenly remembering the surprise. "I must hurry over to Honey Bee Hive."

Teddy went on and soon he came to Honey Bee Hive.

Mr. Honey Bee filled up the red bucket with the very best Mountain Flower Honey. And Teddy carried his bucket home.

But when he got there, Mama Bear wasn't anywhere to be found. Papa Bear wasn't

anywhere, either. And there on Mama Bear's favorite chair sat Cousin Amanda.

When Teddy saw her he wailed, "Where's my mama? I want my mama."

"Oh," said Cousin Amanda, "your mama and papa left here at ten o'clock this morning. They went to visit Grandma and Grandpa Bear. You could have gone with them if you had been back on time."

Teddy Bear ran over to his little soft bed, buried his head under the pine-needle pillow, and cried and cried and cried.

Late that afternoon Mama Bear and Papa Bear came home. Teddy had been thinking. When he saw Mama Bear, he ran to her.

He put his arms around her. "I won't *ever* be a naughty little bear again," he promised.

"Of course you won't," said Mama Bear. "Look what Grandma Bear sent home for you—big chocolate cookies with white sugar frosting. And she wants you to come and see her next week."

And Teddy went.

50

the
enchanted
egg

A FUZZY YELLOW DUCK was the first to find the mysterious egg. He was crossing the green meadow on his way to Pussy Willow Pond for a swim, and there it was lying in the deep grass under a clump of daisies.

"Oh!" he cried, "what a BEAUTIFUL egg!"

He waddled all around it, staring and staring. It was a lovely coral-pink color, with sparkly stars and tiny bluebells painted on it, and bands of squiggly white icing going up and down.

"Now what do you s'pose is inside?" he wondered.

Mrs. Robin was spring cleaning her nest in the old apple tree.

"Come and see the big, beautiful egg!" cried the fuzzy yellow duck.

Mrs. Robin dropped her dust cloth and took off her blue gingham apron. She flew down from the tree top and hopped around the big egg, her bright eyes shining. "Where did it come from?" she asked.

"I don't know," said the fuzzy yellow duck. "It was just here. I think it's an Enchanted Egg!"

"Of course it is," said Mrs. Robin. She picked a buttercup and put it on her head to keep the sun off. "Let's roll it out from

under the daisies," she said. "Then we can see it better."

They squeezed in behind the Enchanted Egg.

"One—Two—Three—GO!" shouted the fuzzy yellow duck, and they each gave a

shove. The egg rolled out into the middle of the sunny meadow. They ran after it, but it didn't stop rolling! It went faster and faster, till it was spinning like a top! Across the meadow it went, through the clover patch and under the honeysuckle hedge!

Beyond the honeysuckle hedge was a long grassy hill. An elf named Dinky lived at the bottom of the hill, in a wee house under a mushroom. And beyond that was the deep pine wood.

ZIP! ZOOM! the egg rolled on down the hill, heading straight for Dinky Elf's wee house under the mushroom!

Dinky was rocking in his little rocking chair, feeling very lonely and wishing that something terribly exciting would happen.

And just as he was wishing, the crash came!

BUMPETY BOOM BANG! The Enchanted Egg struck against the door of Dinky's little house!

"An earthquake!" yelled Dinky. He ran to open his door, but it would not budge!

"An Atom Bomb!" howled Dinky. He ran to open his window. Then he scrambled onto the sill and peeked out.

His front yard was filled with a large pink thing, all glittery in the sunshine! Mrs.

Robin was perched on top, fanning herself
with her buttercup bonnet. A fuzzy yellow
duck was sprawled on the grass, very red in
the face from running.

Dinky jumped down from the window,

landing in the middle of his prize tulips. "Is
it a Flying Saucer?" he shouted.

"Certainly not," said Mrs. Robin. "It's an
Enchanted Egg."

"Oh, how exciting!" cried Dinky. "How

simply terrific!" He bounced up and down with glee. Then he stopped bouncing. "Enchanted means magic," he said, "and if it's magic, it must do something—but WHAT?"

"We don't exactly know," said the fuzzy yellow duck.

"In fact, we don't know AT ALL!" added Mrs. Robin.

Just then Great-Grandmother Owl flapped out from the deep pine wood. She settled down on top of the wee mushroom house and peered at the Enchanted Egg through her bifocal glasses. "Mercy me!" she screeched, "I haven't seen an egg like that since I was a girl! I wonder what picture is inside?"

"PICTURE?" cried Dinky, Mrs. Robin, and the fuzzy yellow duck.

"There are ALWAYS pictures inside of Enchanted Eggs," said Great-Grandmother Owl . . ."little scenes, such as flowers, waterfalls, and fairy palaces! Just roll it over and look in the window!"

So they all pushed and pushed! The Enchanted Egg rolled backwards and they found a little round window with its frame

of squiggly white icing all around it! Everyone crowded up and peered inside.

"Oh, how marvelous! How simply super!" shouted Dinky. "I see a castle with tall towers!"

"I see knights in armor riding white horses!" called the fuzzy yellow duck.

"I see a fairy princess on a balcony," whispered Mrs. Robin.

They looked at the lovely scene for a long time. Then Great-Grandmother Owl said it was time for her to go home.

"If you don't mind, I'd like to stay awhile," said Mrs. Robin wistfully.

"So would I!" said the fuzzy yellow duck.

"Oh, PLEASE do!" cried Dinky. "We'll have a picnic!" He skipped into his wee

house and came back with cookies and milk, and a red-checked tablecloth. Then he spread the cloth on the green lawn beside the Enchanted Egg. "I just love picnics," he

said, "but I've never had one, because I didn't have any friends to invite!"

"And now you've got me!" cried Mrs. Robin.

"And me, too!" quacked the duck.

They sat cross-legged on the lawn and

ate their cookies and milk. And they kept looking at the wonderful picture inside the Enchanted Egg. The knights went on riding their white horses beneath the castle, and the fairy princess looked down from the balcony. Overhead the stars came out one by one. . .

The BUNNY TWINS

There were two little bunnies
With tails round and puffy,
One was named Flipper
And one was named Fluffy.

They woke in the morning
As bright as the sun
And jumped out of bed
With a hop and a run.

They wanted their breakfast
But Mother said, "Dears,
You must first comb your whiskers
And then wash your ears,

"Then dress yourself neatly
As fast as you're able,
While I put the carrots and peas
On the table."

They skipped off to school
    When breakfast was through
With flowers for teacher,
    Some red and some blue.

She taught them to read
And to write and to paint,
And she taught them a bunny
Should never say *ain't*.

When lessons were done
        They were free for the day,
So the twins scampered out
        In the schoolyard to play.

They swung on the swings
   And they slid on the slides,
And when Fluffy got scared
   She hung onto the sides.

But Flipper was brave
As a brother could be,
And he said, "You'll be safe
If you hang onto me."

Then he found a small wagon
And Fluffy climbed in,
While Flip pulled the handle
And gave her a spin.

He galloped so fast
    The cart tipped on its side,
And that was the end
    Of a rollicking ride.

So they hopped up a hillside
And Flip said to Fluff,
"Let's go to our cousins
And play blindman's buff."

There were dozens of cousins,
 Some small and some large,
And Flip made a blindfold,
 And said, "I'll take charge."

He covered his eyes
    And went bouncing around,
Making everyone laugh
    When he fell on the ground.

He was up in a jiffy
   And tagged sister Fluff,
Then the bunnies decided
   They'd played long enough.

So the twins took some skates
With a strap at the back,
And they coasted down hill
Going *clickity-clack*.

Before they could stop
    They rolled over and over,
Like two furry balls
    In a field full of clover.

While they were resting
    Fluff wiggled her toes,
And laughed when a grasshopper
    Tickled her nose.

Then they picked up their skates
And went home in a hurry,
For fear that their mother
Would wonder and worry.

When they got to the door
Mother hugged them
and kissed them,
To show the twin bunnies
How much she had missed them!